Quit BEING AN Idiot

LIFE LESSONS
from

The Golden Girls

ROBB PEARLMAN

HYPERION
AVENUE
LOS ANGELES   NEW YORK

First Edition, September 2023
10 9 8 7 6 5 4 3 2 1
FAC-034274-23215
Printed in the United States of America

This book is set in Futura and Lust
Designed by Amy C. King

Library of Congress Control Number: 2023931545
ISBN 978-1-368-07766-8
Reinforced binding

www.HyperionAvenueBooks.com

Introduction

SOPHIA: Picture it: Miami . . . a house, the only one in the neighborhood without a pool. But I digress. Four women, friends. They laugh, they cry, they eat. They love, they hate, they eat. They dream, they hope, they eat. Every time you turn around, they eat.

ROSE: Sophia, are those four women us?

SOPHIA: Look in the mirror, blubber butt. The point I'm trying to make is, what's going on here is living. Just because you have some rough times doesn't mean you throw in the towel. You go on living. And eating.

When the opening credits of *The Golden Girls* rolled across television screens into homes across the country in 1985 for the first time, they heralded something viewers had never seen before: a sitcom focused on women over the age of fifty. Created by Susan Harris and starring television stalwarts Beatrice Arthur (as Dorothy), Rue McClanahan (as Blanche), and Betty White (as Rose), and featuring character actress Estelle Getty (as Sophia), the Miami-set show was an immediate success, winning multiple Emmys and legions of fans across the world.

Because *The Golden Girls* was so packed with memorable characters, stories, and quotable moments, it was, and remains, one of the few shows enjoyed by so many demographics that it proved seemingly disparate audiences had a lot more in common than they (or anyone) thought. The show, which is still enjoyed by millions, was a lot more than entertainment. For the entirety of its seven seasons, *The Golden Girls* taught us how to laugh—but it also taught us a number of lessons about life. At a time when few other shows were even *trying* to discuss important, real-life issues, the Girls were never afraid to pull up a chair, share a slice of cheesecake, and talk about whatever was on their minds. In fact, thanks in very large part to audiences seeing how spirited and downright sexy Dorothy, Blanche, Rose, and Sophia were, "over the age of fifty" no longer means "old."

Each character contributed something indescribable to the alchemical reaction that made each episode so much more than the sum of its parts. As described by Laszlo, the sculptor, in the Season 3 episode "The Artist," "Why not take the best features of each lady to create one perfect lady? . . . You know, it is not hard to understand why you are such good friends; you complement each other very well indeed." So even though they may have had opposing views on many things, Dorothy, Blanche, Rose, and even Sophia found common ground to grow, love, and laugh together.

The Golden Girls was a fun, funny, and celebratory guide for how everyone could lead a rich, full, and authentic life. The show taught us how to fill a home with love, and how to put our parents away in one. It showed us that not everyone looks bad in vacuum slacks, and that not everyone looks good in a backless dress. It proved that though stories may bind us, adding sugary cereal to a pasta sauce may have a different effect. It demonstrated, in words and action, that you can write your phone number on the windshield of a Chrysler LeBaron using nothing but the heel of your Pappagallo pump, that you never want to wind up as a St. Olaf story, and that friendship, laughter, and cheesecake are all you need. The lessons that the Girls illuminated are just as applicable anywhere in the world today as they were on a lanai in Miami back in 1985.

Got it? Now quit being an idiot and read this book!

You're the Best!

ROSE: I haven't added anything to the world.

SOPHIA: Look, Rose. God doesn't make mistakes. We were all put on this planet for a purpose. Blanche, you're here to work in a museum so that art can be appreciated by humanity. Dorothy, you're here as a substitute teacher to educate our youth. And, Rose, you're here because the rhythm method was very popular in the twenties.

hough you can spend hours deciding if you're a Dorothy, Blanche, Rose, or Sophia, you need to remember that there is nobody—nobody—like you. (Unless you happen to be Jorge and Esteban, the passionate and virtually interchangeable twins from the Jimmy Smits look-alike contest, but chances are you are not.)

When Rose discovers she's been nominated for the St. Olaf Woman of the Year award, she sets out to write down a list of her accomplishments. Disappointed to have achieved so little (in her mind), she gives up and goes back to bed. Dorothy and Blanche think that she's a poor judge of herself, though, and take it upon themselves to send in a slightly embellished application on her behalf. Rose is thrilled to learn that she's won, even beating out local heroine Emma Immerhoffer, who manages an orphanage, takes in the homeless, and runs a soup kitchen. But later she is devastated to learn that she's done so under *slightly* false pretenses. She refuses to accept the award and barely speaks to Dorothy and Blanche on their way home.

Rose eventually forgives them. She understands that they were just trying to help, and as friends who have eaten over five hundred cheesecakes together, they were, perhaps, in a better position to see just how special she is. Even if they are chronic two-faced liars. So, when you're feeling down, look to your friends to remind you of how much you've accomplished, how much you are valued, and how much you are loved.

Cheesecake Is Powerful

DOROTHY: Do you know how many problems we have solved over a cheesecake at this kitchen table?

ROSE: No. Exactly how many?

DOROTHY: One hundred and forty-seven, Rose!

Gathering around a table to share a meal, stories, and your time will nourish your stomach and your soul.

A lanai is great for a cookout. A living room is perfect for watching TV, practicing some dirty dancing moves, or recuperating from the flu. But the best place in the house, where the Golden Girls had countless great late-night talks (mostly about sex) was the kitchen. It was around the kitchen table where they ate leftovers, ice cream sundaes, pasta, and, of course, cheesecake. The kitchen is where they consoled each other, helped each other, advised each other, and then talked about sex again. Food, as a love language, brought these four women and their guests together in ways none of them could have imagined. It was through food, and during their shared meals, that they experienced their families' and cultures' traditions, attempted restraint (by counting calories), indulged in treats to make themselves and each other feel better, and ensured they were all getting the physical and emotional strength they needed.

Instead of hurrying through a meal to do something else, try slowing down, savoring the food, and the company, as much as you can. Food will spoil, but your memories of breaking bread, and cheesecake crust, with your friends will last forever.

Math Is Hard, Especially When It Comes to Age

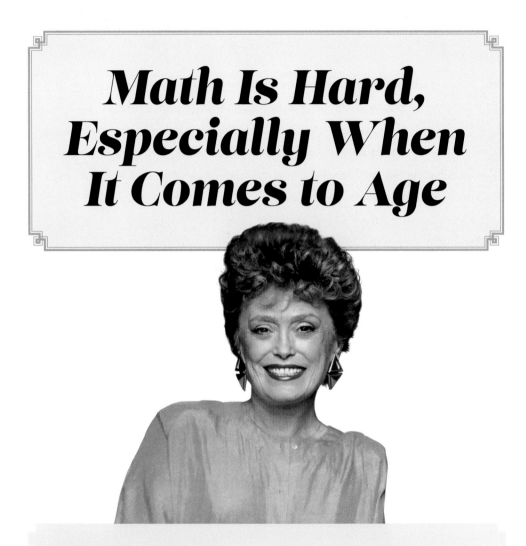

BLANCHE: There are lots of ways you can trick a man into thinkin' you're younger than you really are. You wear sunglasses, put on a little extra makeup, go to dimly lit restaurants.

ROSE: We've all done that.

BLANCHE: Fly to Nevada to get a fake birth certificate. Have a phony high school yearbook printed up. Change the dates on your parents' graves.

DOROTHY: We've all done that.

*I*t's impossible to stay forty-nine forever. Even in dog years.

As happy as Blanche is to hear that Jason, the leading man in the play, thinks her audition went well, she's even happier to hear that he also thinks her granddaughter Aurora is her daughter. She and Jason start dating, and to continue the illusion, Blanche offers (insists) on babysitting all the time. Though Rebecca's shocked by her mother's newfound interest in Aurora, the Girls know that their friend is selfishly using the baby to appear younger than she is. When Blanche finally admits the truth, she loses Jason, and almost loses her family.

Though it may be possible to stave off some of the traditional physical and mental signs of aging, it's impossible to stop the clock at any one point in time. Unless you die, you are going to get older, though you don't have to get old. Accept and be proud of your age!

Friends Help You Through

SOPHIA: It's not whether you agree or disagree with somebody. It's whether you can be there for that person when they need you.

good friend will be there for you when no one else is, even if they have to cancel a hot date.

While Sophia is naturally upset after leaving her friend Lydia's funeral—and not just because they were wearing the same dress—her other friend, Martha, is inconsolable over the loss. A day later, Martha invites Sophia to a fancy dinner to show off her brand-new attitude *and* brand-new plan. Martha, determined not to go through the pain and suffering that Lydia did at the end, has decided to take her own life.

Sophia is shocked, even more so when she's asked to be present and holding Martha's hand at the end. Sophia finds herself in the untenable position of either helping her friend do something she doesn't agree with or abandoning her in her time of need. But Sophia offers Martha—and herself—a viable third option: a reaffirmation of their friendship and a commitment to find a way through this particularly dark time *together*.

Sometimes the limits of a friendship are tested harder than a pile of hotel towels test the rivets on a suitcase. Remember that good friendships, the ones that matter, are bolted together like a clamshell telephone attached to a side table.

Get to the Point

ROSE: I don't know, I think it's impossible to paint autumn in St. Olaf.

DOROTHY: How come?

ROSE: Maybe it's because of the horrible St. Olaf falling-leaf story.

DOROTHY: Please, Rose, if this a story about a man named Leif, I don't want to hear it.

ROSE: It's not that long.

DOROTHY: No.

ROSE: It has a surprise ending.

DOROTHY: All right, Rose, just the ending, but keep it short!

ROSE: . . . Splat.

The only thing better than telling a story, especially a St. Olaf story, is telling a short story.

Stories should be purposeful, brief, and, preferably, told over cheesecake. So keep it short.

Real short.

Like, Sophia-short.

Always Be Honest, Even if It Hurts

DOROTHY: Okay, girls, which goes better, the silver chain or the pearls?

ROSE: The chain.

BLANCHE: An amateur's mistake. Can't you see that the chain accentuates the many folds of that turkey-like neck?

ROSE: Well, that may be, but the pearls draw attention to the nonexistent bosom.

BLANCHE: Yes, but the chain leads the eye even lower to that huge spare tire jutting out over those square, manly hips.

DOROTHY: Why don't I just wear a sign that says "Too ugly to live"?

BLANCHE: Fine, but what are you gonna hang it from, the chain or the pearls?

DOROTHY: Neither! I'm gonna spray-paint it on my hump!

There are lots of people in your life who will tell you what you want to hear. A true friend will tell you what you *need* to hear. Even if it's as painful as running face-first into a crossing signal as the train carrying your boyfriend speeds down the tracks.

After Sophia's last friend, Bernice, moves back to Chicago, she finds herself adrift and lonely. The Girls tell her a hard truth: She needs to go out and make new friends. Dorothy tries to make things easier by inviting Sophia to join her and her new boyfriend, Raymond, on their dates. Despite having the best of intentions, Dorothy soon faces regret and a strained relationship with Raymond when Sophia becomes a constant and intrusive third wheel. Things come to a stressful head when Dorothy has to tell Sophia she can't go on a Bahamas trip she's invited herself on. Dorothy must, as a daughter, and a friend, be honest with Sophia, even if it hurts her mother's feelings and stresses both of them out. Unlike Blanche and Rose, who jump at the opportunity to explain to Dorothy, in excruciating detail, why she should reconsider ever leaving the house again, given her "less-than" appearance, Dorothy herself struggles to find the right time to tell Sophia the truth about her behavior.

When Dorothy finally works up the courage to have what is sure to be a difficult and painful conversation, Sophia explains that she's made other plans and will not join her on their vacation.

Though we may not all be as fortunate to have the edges of difficult conversations softened by eavesdropping or turns of fate, we must still be willing and able to be honest with our friends, even if the truth of a situation will, for a time, hurt.

Love Expands, It Does Not Replace

SOPHIA: Look, Charlie loved you for over thirty years. But he's gone now, and you've met someone you really care about. What do you think Charlie would say?

ROSE: I think he'd say he loves me.

SOPHIA: And what about the ring?

ROSE: He'd probably say it was okay to wear Miles's ring because Miles can love me in a way that he can't right now.

*U*nlike the weight you lose through the St. Olaf "I can't believe this is cheese" diet, the loss of a loved one can be so devastating it is hard to see how to move forward, let alone how another relationship could ever be achieved.

Farm girl Rose is thrilled when her college professor boyfriend Miles gives her a ring . . . more than a friendship ring, but not quite an engagement ring. Subsequently, she's shocked when she opens the refrigerator to find that, somehow, all the cantaloupe is off to the side of the fruit salad. An arrangement of fruit that is the clear signal she and Charlie arranged before his death—a sign that he had a message for her from beyond the grave. Rose assumes—as anyone with experience interpreting fruit would—that Charlie doesn't want her to be with another man. After some ill-intended manipulation of Rose's feelings, Sophia realizes that Rose is letting her guilt and loyalty to Charlie, and his memory, keep her from being happy. Eventually, she helps Rose see the light (and not just the one the little man in the refrigerator shuts on and off) and understand that Charlie would want her to move on with love and life.

It's extraordinarily difficult to open yourself up to finding love and happiness after the loss of a partner, especially if that loss was unexpected and sudden. Remember that if they truly loved you—and they did—they believed that you deserved, and still deserve, love.

Get a Good Night's Sleep

BLANCHE: What day is this? I've been up for seventy-two hours. I had a breakthrough. I discovered a new form of writing. I will go down in history. First I wrote all day, then I tore it all up, and then that night it came to me, and the words poured forth like liquid from a stream. It was almost a mystical experience. Somebody else was writing this.

ROSE: Who?

BLANCHE: Everyman. This is everyman's work. It's all gold. Just open it anywhere and the magic will touch you. But I'm so tired. I must sleep. And I cannot sleep. I am too tired to sleep. I will never sleep again. I may die from this. What am I gonna do?

*I*f you weren't pretty in college, you probably pulled an all-nighter or two. Unfortunately, you're now way, *way* too mature for matriculation. So get some rest.

While Dorothy tries to discover why she's been exhausted for months, Blanche exhausts herself to fulfill the destiny set out for her by her mother: to become great. And because one should always write what they know, she decides to become a great romance novelist. She wants to carry on in the tradition of other great Southern writers . . . the ones who are so famous they need not be mentioned. She won't even have to use her imagination—her life is a romance novel (not a sports page, as Sophia suggests).

But as fate would have it, words do not come tripping onto the page as quickly or easily as dew on a honeysuckle, and Blanche faces a severe case of writer's block. Though she stays up all night in a pique of literary artistry, she quickly realizes that the absolute gibberish she's jotted down overnight is . . . just too good to sell to a publisher. They can publish it after she's dead, just like van Gogh! Unlike van Gogh, she has too many earrings to only have one ear.

Most people underestimate the importance of getting a good night's sleep. Side effects of sleep deprivation include road accidents, loss of concentration, headaches, or mistaking a bag of egg yolks for a collection of little balls of sunshine. Go to bed (and we don't mean simply to **B**lanche **E**lizabeth **D**everaux).

Some People Are Just Mean

ROSE: How can you hate a living thing?

MRS. CLAXTON: I hate you.

You never know what someone is going through, so it's important to always be kind. It's also important to recognize that a select few people are actually rather rotten human beings.

The Girls are on a mission to save the two-hundred-year-old oak tree on Mrs. Claxton's property. Though they've received signatures from sixty residents of Richmond Street, they haven't gotten one very important person to sign up: Mrs. Claxton herself. Unlike Ernest T. Minky, St. Olaf's librarian/dentist, who only needed to be shown a little kindness to be kind himself, Mrs. Claxton's attitude cannot be swayed by Rose's optimism or any amount of homemade Danish. Mrs. Claxton hates everyone, and in turn, everyone hates Mrs. Claxton. When Rose finally sees Mrs. Claxton for the miserable vile scum-sucking crank that she is, she tells the woman that she's no longer going to try to waste time kissing her fanny, and if she doesn't like what they have to say, she can just drop dead. Finally, Mrs. Claxton agrees, so she does. Drop dead, that is.

This isn't the first time Rose has been at least tangentially the cause of someone's death, so she's once again racked with guilt, especially when nobody attends Mrs. Claxton's funeral. But Rose has the last laugh—and sweet revenge on her neighbor—when she finds the perfect final resting place for Mrs. Claxton's cremated ashes: at the base of the tree in dispute. Not only does this save the tree from demolition, it also proves that her life had meaning: as fertilizer and as a target for any dog passing by.

Some people just have no use for other people. They're alone and miserable because they want to be. So stay out of their way as best as you can and afford them the respect that is due. Which may be none. In which case call her a garconanokin* and be done with it.

*Literally, the precise moment when dog doo turns white, but in general, it refers to the kind of person you don't want to share your hoogencoggles with.

Friends Are the Best Teachers

DOROTHY: Well, we've all learned a lot from each other. I mean, Ma taught me life does not end because you've reached a certain age. And I've become much more comfortable with my sexuality because of Blanche. And Rose has taught me . . . Rose has taught me . . .

LUCAS: It's not important.

DOROTHY: No, wait, no, I can do this. Rose has taught me . . .

LUCAS: Let it go.

DOROTHY: I need some time with this. Anyway, because of them I feel that I'm ready to love you—A square knot! Rose taught me how to tie a square knot.

It can be as impossible to quantify the ways a friend can enrich your life as it is impossible to describe the most interesting things about the tar business.

Though Dorothy was the only licensed substitute teacher of the group, the house at 6151 Richmond Street might as well have been designated an institute of higher learning by the Greater Miami School District. Blanche taught Sophia how, with a new outfit and some makeup, she could go from looking like an eighty-four-year-old woman to a sixty-five-year-old drag queen. Rose taught the Girls the difference between hide-and-seek and Oogle and Foogle. Sophia taught the Girls how to get a free bottle of champagne and the 152 ingredients in salsa grandioso. As friends—as family—the Girls taught one another how to get over heartbreak, how to enjoy the small moments in life, and how to install a toilet. In the end, they taught each other how to say goodbye.

By sharing your life with your friends, you are taught and, in turn, *teach* in immeasurable and countless ways.

Love Is Love Is Lanai

BLANCHE: Oh look, I can accept the fact that he's gay, but why does he have to slip a ring on this guy's finger so the whole world will know?

SOPHIA: Why did you marry George?

BLANCHE: We loved each other. We wanted to make a lifetime commitment. Wanted everybody to know.

SOPHIA: That's what Doug and Clayton want, too. Everyone wants someone to grow old with. And shouldn't everyone have that chance?

QUIT BEING AN IDIOT

espite the enormous steps society has taken toward equality in the last few decades, there will still be people who don't understand how cathartic empathy can be. (If you don't know what that means, just try repeating it to look smarter than you actually are: "Was it cathartic?" "Oh, I've had a catharticism." "Of course, I'm not the type to kiss and catharticize.") But I digress. By trying to understand, appreciate, and accept someone else's feelings and experiences, we allow ourselves to grow and expand our own capacity to love.

Blanche has a lot more in common with her brother Clayton than she thinks. It turns out that besides being great-looking and charming, they're both irresistible to men. In addition to needing to confront her feelings about Clayton's sexual orientation, she also needs to confront her feelings about their relationship. Though she may have momentarily questioned whether she really knew her brother, Blanche never questions how much she loves him.

Later, when Clayton introduces the Girls to his "special friend" Doug, Blanche has to confront her feelings about two external relationships: Clayton and Doug's relationship, and what society at large would say about it. Blanche's objection to their upcoming marriage is not (entirely) selfish. It is born out of love and the deep need to shield her brother, and his fiancé, from harm. She knows, as we all do, that as much as LGBTQ+ folks can be warmly welcomed by friends and family, they can often face cruelty from strangers. Sophia—a devout Catholic— demonstrated, through compassion, empathy, and patience, and Blanche's own shared experience, that Clayton and Doug's love is no less important, sacred, or worthy of celebration than the one she shared with George.

Your experiences and feelings are no more or less worthy than anyone else's. Though you may not fully understand or relate to someone else's life, it is incumbent upon you—as a fellow human being—to not diminish or discount them. Everyone deserves the chance to grow old with someone. So mind your own business.

Still Waters Run Deep

DOROTHY: The slut is dead. Long live the slut.

*I*sn't it wonderful that even after years of friendship your friends can do or say things about themselves that can surprise—even *stun*—you?

Rose's old boyfriend, Thor Anderson from St. Olaf, is coming to Miami and wants to talk about old times. The problem is, Rose doesn't know any Thor Andersons from St. Olaf. And after two dates, she still has no recollection.

Blanche questions how a naive farmer's daughter like Rose could not remember a boyfriend (*boyfriend* defined by Blanche as any man you bring to a fevered pitch of uncontrollable ecstasy). It does make sense, though, considering that Rose had fifty-six boyfriends before getting married. *Fifty-six.* She would have had more but she wasn't allowed to date until she was a senior in high school. Much to everyone's surprise, and with alarming speed, the simple farm girl from St. Olaf has quickly replaced the Southern belle with multiple "first-time stories" as the resident tramp.

Sometimes friends keep things from one another for good reasons. Other times, they either simply forget to mention something or just don't think it's important. Rather than feeling bad about not knowing something about your friend's past, revel in the fact that you can still learn, and love, something new about those closest to you.

Side Hustles May Cost More Than They Earn

SOPHIA: Rose, let me give you a few lessons in economics.
Lesson number one: Quit being an idiot. . . .
Lesson number two: The law of supply and demand. Before you supply the sandwiches, you demand the money. . . .
Lesson number three: Quit being an idiot.

ven if you have a regular, well-paying nine-to-five job, an extra freelance or part-time gig can offer a few extra dollars in your wallet, and a chance to meet construction workers at the crack of dawn. But that doesn't always mean it's worth it.

When Sophia and Rose decide to start a business selling bacon, lettuce, and potato sandwiches to hungry construction workers, they're prepared to get up early, spend time making and selling the food, and pad their bank accounts. What they don't expect to face is a rivalry with another lunch wagoner named Johnny No Thumbs and, worst of all, failure to turn a profit. After some introspection, a late-night visit from Johnny's business associates, Vinnie and Rocco, and a review of their books, they decide to get out of the sandwich game.

It's easy, especially in today's gig economy and work-from-home culture to try to take on a second or even third job. But before you take on the added responsibilities, try to figure out if you're going to lose sleep, money, and fingers.

You Only Get One Chance to Make a Last Impression

ROSE: Sophia, wills are no joking matter. Charlie tried to be funny with his and left everything to Henrietta, our prized cow. Well, some lawyer got ahold of the will and represented Henrietta on contingency. There I was presenting my side to a jury of her peers. It took over six months to get the farm back.

SOPHIA: What a terrible story. I mean it. It's a terrible story. But you must have been relieved when you won.

ROSE: Oh yeah. We celebrated with a big, thick steak.

Though it may visit Shady Pines more often than some other locations, hardly anybody anywhere wants to talk about death, much less plan for it.

Much like Rose had to confront the reality of her will with her daughter, Kirsten, Sophia feels, now that she's getting on in years, it's finally time to settle her estate and enlists Rose (of all people) to help create an ironclad will. Because Dorothy thinks the entirety of Sophia's bequest would be a loofa sponge, bus pass, and the four gold teeth Sal stole while working at a funeral parlor, she's willing to indulge their legal planning sessions. But when Rose inadvertently violates their attorney-client privilege and discloses the fact that there's also $35,000 (over $120,000 in today's money), Dorothy is livid. While *she's* been scrimping, saving, and sacrificing to keep a roof over their heads, her sister has been sending Sophia money for the last ten years. With the money Dorothy might have saved, she could have had her own condo instead of living with a slut and a moron. (Her words, not ours!)

After a while, Dorothy realizes that she likes taking care of Sophia but wishes her mother had been honest about the money. Sophia, in turn, admits that it was never about the money—she feels that she'd be a nobody if she didn't leave her children anything. She wants her kids, especially Dorothy, to have everything they want when she's gone so they can look back and say, "I have this because of Ma." Dorothy reminds her mother that life isn't just valued by the money people leave, it's the memories and the love that matter.

Remember to plan, as best you can, so your friends and family don't have to deal with a significant financial burden, and to make sure the things you love make their way to the people you love. Beyond that, think about the truly important things that people will treasure: the intangible moments, the deep feelings, the shared experiences, and the laughs.

Practice Patience

BLANCHE: Rose, what were you doing out so early this morning?

ROSE: Well, I couldn't sleep, so I went for a spin last night. To Alabama. Blanche, do you know at a truck stop in Tuscaloosa they have an egg dish named after you.

BLANCHE: Really? How are they prepared?

SOPHIA: Over easy.

he only thing more difficult than waiting is convincing your husband that it was good for you, too.

Time seems to stand still when Rose gets a letter from St. Luke's Hospital. She needs to get a test to make sure that the transfusion she received during her gallbladder surgery didn't contain HIV antibodies. She schedules the test immediately but is surprised to learn that she must wait three days to get the results. During that time, Rose begins to worry, lose sleep, and lash out in frustration and fear. Lucky for Rose, she has her friends to help her through. When Rose asks Blanche how she handled waiting for her own test results, Blanche tells her that she kept it to herself and just acted like a real bitch to everyone else. Which explains why nobody sensed a change in her attitude. And she's able to laugh, at least a little, with Dorothy, who knows it's been a bad week for Rose but that as long as they're together, it'll get better.

Time may seem to drag when you're waiting for news, or speed up when you're having fun. It can also make the time you have left seem so much longer when you're stuck at home completing a jigsaw puzzle with a fifty-five-year-old daughter who's cramping your social life. It's important to remember to savor the good times, be patient with the things that simply cannot be rushed, and know that the best way to spend your time is with those you love.

We're All Trying Our Best

DOROTHY: We all make the best decisions we can make with what we know.

*L*ife is filled with difficult choices. Some, like choosing the right breast implants, can be solved by comparing and contrasting photos laid out on a coffee table. Others, however, require split-second, and not always perfect, decisions.

Even after forty years, Dorothy never forgave John Noretti for standing her up the night of their prom. It destroyed her self-esteem and drove her into the arms of another man. Well, not his *arms* exactly. More into the backseat of his car. It's only when Dorothy comes face-to-face with John, and the truth, that she learns what happened: Sophia hadn't thought John was dressed or behaved properly enough for her little girl, and so she sent him away.

Though Sophia apologizes, Dorothy can't understand how her mother could have made such a unilateral and life-changing decision on her behalf. John, however, offers Dorothy another perspective on that night: He's grateful to Sophia for driving him to grow up and become a better version of himself. In the end, Dorothy understands that Sophia did the best she could with the tools and language she had at the time. Not only did Sophia have no experience raising a teenaged daughter, but the resources and communication skills available to her as a young mother were vastly different from what's available to modern parents.

They say hindsight is 20/20, but they often fail to mention it's only 20/20 if you can find your glasses. As we get older and gain more experience, it's natural to look back on the decisions that we made, and the decisions that were made for us, in a different light. Remember that we all do the best we can with the tools, language, and information we have at the time. Try to be kind to yourself, and others, for not always making the right choices.

Personal Gifts Are Best

BLANCHE: Girls, I wanna give you all my gifts next, okay? I just thought this was such a cute idea, I made the same one for each of you. Here, Sophia.

ROSE: "The Men of Blanche's Boudoir."

BLANCHE: It's a calendar. Each month has the picture of a man who's brought some special joy into my life.

DOROTHY: Oh, Blanche. Oh, honey. This is so thoughtful. Whoa!

BLANCHE: September?

DOROTHY: Yep.

SOPHIA: I'm surprised you were able to walk in October.

The holidays are a time of peace, joy, and overspending.

After Sophia uses Dorothy's credit cards to buy Blanche a cashmere sweater and Rose a video recorder, Dorothy laments that everyone thinks the best way to show they care about others is by going into debt. When Dorothy searches her heart for the true spirit of Christmas, Sophia suggests it can be found in ladies' apparel on the third floor of Neiman Marcus. In an effort to calm Dorothy, save money, and enjoy the holiday before they all travel away to celebrate Christmas with their families, Rose suggests the Girls have a St. Olaf–style Christmas: Rather than buying gifts for one another, the residents of Rose's hometown exchange handmade, heartfelt gifts. Though Sophia is resistant, Blanche and Dorothy are on board with the plan and agree to return all the meaningless impersonal gifts they'd bought for one another and instead create their own treasures.

Rose whittles them maple-syrup spigots, which are perfect for anyone who is lost in the woods with a stack of pancakes. Not to be outdone, Blanche gifts the Girls calendars featuring photos of her most memorable gentlemen callers. Filled with images that are at once emotionally and physically exciting, it's the sort of handmade, thoughtful gift that can be enjoyed throughout the year. Just like Blanche.

Spending money on store-bought presents cannot compete with spending time with family and friends, telling stories about an all-chicken version of *A Christmas Carol*, and exchanging gifts that you've put real thought, effort, and creativity into. Warm experiences and heartfelt gestures are the true gifts.

Get Second and Third Opinions

ROSE: Doctors don't know everything, Dorothy.

DOROTHY: You're right.

ROSE: I mean, they think they do, but they don't.

DOROTHY: You're right.

ROSE: I mean, after all, Dr. Seuss was a doctor, too.

The only thing worse than being sick *isn't* looking sick (though that's really, really terrible); it's being made to feel that it's all in your head.

Every doctor is quick to dismiss the five months of Dorothy's sore throat, swollen glands, fever, and extreme exhaustion as psychosomatic. Rather than running tests, they—especially the particularly condescending Dr. Budd— advise her that she's just getting older, and suggest that she date more, see a psychiatrist, take a cruise, or change her hair color.

Despondent, Dorothy begins to question if there is anything truly the matter with her at all. In a last-ditch effort, and to quell Sophia's fears that she's dying of something that no one has ever heard of before, she goes to see their friend and neighbor, empty nester Dr. Harry Weston. He believes Dorothy's self-report and refers her to a virologist on staff at his hospital, who gives her some gratifying, if sober, news: Dorothy may have the (then relatively unknown) disease known as chronic fatigue syndrome. As she sits down with the Girls for a dinner celebrating finally being able to name what's wrong with her, Dorothy spots Dr. Budd in the restaurant and gives him a piece of her mind, noting that should *he* ever be in the scared, vulnerable position that she was in, she hopes he finds a doctor who treats him better than he treated her. Turning heel, Dorothy leaves him to deal with his cold dinner, and furious wife.

Doctors and health care providers take an oath to do no harm. Although they, unfortunately, must sometimes deliver news their patients don't want to hear, they should always treat them with patience, kindness, respect, and compassion. If you ever find yourself in the position where you feel otherwise, you are entitled to a second, or even third, opinion.

Get Ready, Freddy– Because You Deserve It!

UNCLE LUCAS: Gonna be a great honeymoon. Me, Dorothy, and Freddy Peterson.

Sex is great, but it's even better when you have a deep and meaningful connection with your partner. And if the sex isn't great, give it two more dates just to make sure.

For all intents and purposes, Dorothy's relationship with Stanley began with sex. Sex that was as unsatisfying as their marriage and fraught with as many unexpected consequences as their divorce. Later, her years of dating presented her with many highs (a clown, a married teacher, a fake Beatle) and lows (Stanley!), and intimacy and sex remained challenging for her. It was only after years of witnessing Blanche own *her* sexuality and Rose committing to love, not to mention building her own self-confidence and independence, that Dorothy found though sex, love, and confidence are all nice on their own, they are even better together. So, it is a surprise to everyone—especially Dorothy—when her romance with Blanche's uncle Lucas started as a joke but blossomed into love. It was that love, trust, and maturity that, in turn, laid the foundation for a sex life so fulfilling and unique that they had no choice and named it . . . Freddy Peterson.

By loving yourself, knowing what you want (and what you don't), and working through the issues that are keeping you from experiencing pleasure, sex can provide the fun, silly, passionate, carefree, wistful, and romantic feelings of enjoyment everyone deserves.

Accept, and Respect, People for Who They Are

SOPHIA: Jean is a lesbian.

BLANCHE: What's funny about that?

SOPHIA: You aren't surprised?

BLANCHE: Of course not. I mean, I've never known any personally, but isn't Danny Thomas one?

DOROTHY: Not Lebanese, Blanche. Lesbian.

Some people like girls. Some like guys. Some people like cats instead of dogs. Everyone deserves the respect, support, and love you would want yourself.

Unsure about how they'll react to the news, and probably wary about disclosing someone else's personal information, Dorothy decides not to tell Blanche and Rose that her friend Jean is a lesbian. Though they are all able to keep Jean's sexuality a private matter, things take a queer turn when Jean starts developing romantic feelings for Rose. While Blanche is shocked more at the fact that Jean would be attracted to Rose and not her, Rose is shocked that their quick friendship has, from Jean's perspective, developed into something different. Still, rather than being upset, uncomfortable, or judgmental about Jean and her affection, Rose is honored to be thought of in that way. Because she can't reciprocate the romantic feelings Jean has for her, Rose offers what she can: that they remain friends—as long as that was enough for Jean. Rose was honest about her own feelings and boundaries while, at the same time, showing kindness, respect, and acceptance of Jean as a person.

Everyone has their own process for disclosing personal information about themselves. Some information will come as a surprise. Some won't. And, sometimes, things are just so matter-of-fact and mundane that they barely register at all. Regardless of anything else, the golden path is to treat people with the respect that everyone deserves.

Keep Busy

ROSE: Sophia, why are you in such a bad mood?

SOPHIA: Forgive me, Rose, but I haven't had sex in fifteen years and it's starting to get on my nerves.

*I*t's important, especially as you get older, to stay engaged, possibly stimulated, or at least as excited as one is when winning the annual St. Olaf Me-and-My-Pet-Look-Alike contest.

With the possible exception of the paycheck that comes with it, the only good thing about work is that it might allow you to channel your passion about a particular subject or goal into a satisfying and meaningful career. Whether it's because of retirement or the cancellation of ladies' night at the Rusty Anchor, many may find fewer opportunities for fulfillment as they age.

All the Girls were able to channel their interests and passions into a wide variety of activities that, if nothing else, served to keep them vibrant and active. When Blanche felt she needed to abstain from making love, she found pleasure, and calories, in making things out of Popsicle sticks. Dorothy coached a kids' football team and attended a wide variety of symposiums. Rose volunteered more than anyone, except for Agnes Bradshaw. And though nobody knew it, Sophia filled her days by volunteering in a hospital, conducting a jazz band, and buying a nectarine. Or there was always just watching television or cleaning out their closets.

Taking up a hobby, attending adult education classes, traveling, volunteering, or even just occasionally meeting up with Mel Bushman are all ideal ways for you to keep your mind and, if you're lucky, your hands, busy.

You'll Always Remember Your First Time

BLANCHE: Well, I certainly didn't wait for my wedding night, honey. I couldn't. I had these urges. You know, in the South, we mature faster. I think it's the heat.

DOROTHY: I think it's the gin.

BLANCHE: Anyhow, my first was Billy. Oh, I remember it so well, just like it was yesterday. That night under the dogwood trees, the air thick with perfume, and me with Billy. Or Bobby. Yeah, Bobby. Yeah, it was Bobby. Or was it Ben? Oh, who knows? Anyway, it started with a *B*.

*H*aving sex for the first time is a big deal. Though you may not remember exactly how it physically felt, you'll almost certainly remember how it made you feel emotionally, and how your breasts looked in the moonlight.

Losing your virginity is, for many, a milestone that signifies entry into adulthood. Each of the Girls lost her virginity in her own unique way. Rose's first encounter was with Charlie on their wedding night. Though she was surprised at how he compared to the bull she once saw (the bull would be jealous), she most remembered how nice it was to be so close to him. Dorothy recalled how she went to a drive-in with Stanley, who told her he was being shipped off to Korea. Eager to contribute to the war effort, she wasn't sure anything had actually happened until their son was born nine months later. Blanche, for her part, had too many first-time stories to keep the details straight, but the one unalterable part of the story was that she was finally able to act on the urges that had been building for years.

When contemplating having sex for the first time, think about who you're with, where you are, and the reasons you're doing it. The emotional and mental memories, images, and associations will last far, far longer than the three seconds it took Stan.

Book Smarts Only Get You So Far

DOROTHY: I'm not staying for dinner tonight. There's a meeting at Mensa. That's the organization for people with high IQs like mine.

ROSE: You know, in St. Olaf we had a chapter of Mensa, and across the room was Girlsa. No, wait, those were the bathrooms at St. Olaf's only Italian restaurant.

en go to night school. Smart men. And there's nothing more alluring than a smart man. Unless it's a stupid one with good hands.

All the Golden Girls placed a value on education. Blanche fondly remembers her college campus bursting with green lawns and willow trees and young men, like Ham Lushbough, in chinos and ties, and professors with just a touch of gray at their temples. The professor leaned over your books with you and you smelled his pipe tobacco and his maleness. Then the professor's arm accidentally brushed against your bosoms and the room was filled with the heat of taboo lust. . . .

Anyhow . . . Without technically having a high school diploma, Rose drew the right straw and thus was valedictorian of her high school class, giving a speech entitled "There's a Big World Out There but You Have to Change Buses in Tyler's Landing if You Want to See It," and going on to become a sister in Sigma Yam.

Though she didn't have much of a formal education, Sophia passed on the opportunity while at Shady Pines to go to college, realizing it was just code for allowing the administration to presell her body to the medical school.

Yet it was Dorothy, the first member of her family to attend college, and who achieved enough academically to be certified as a substitute teacher, who was the most proud of her educational accomplishments. So much so that it came as a surprise to her when she felt stupid compared to the high school honors students she was teaching. To boost her spirits, Sophia tells Dorothy that when she was twelve she was named the brightest kid in Brooklyn. Feeling validated, Dorothy takes her elevated sense of self-importance a bit too far and begins to distance herself from everyone else. When Sophia reveals that she lied to her about her high IQ in much the same way she's lied to her for over sixty years about Santa Claus, the Easter Bunny, and other things, Dorothy is brought back down to reality, and remembers that book smarts are useless without being able to connect to other people.

Colleges and trade schools offer people of all ages the opportunity to advance their education, career prospects, and intellectual pursuits. Remember that it is our emotional intelligence, our ability to communicate and relate to others, that truly provides for a happy and well-rounded life.

Tough Love Is Tough

SOPHIA: She screamed, she hollered, day and night. She made me do my therapy. She forced me to rebuild my life because she knew I could. And for that I'll always be grateful.

DOROTHY: Oh, thanks, Ma.

SOPHIA: I only have one question. Now that I'm better, why do you still scream and holler at me?

*I*f you want a spy to talk, you should force them to grade junior high English essays. Sometimes, if you want to help your friends and family in their time of need, the best, most loving thing you can do is to let them—or *force* them—to help themselves.

Rose's sister Lily has recently lost her sight. It's because she's always been an accomplished, independent woman that she can't come to grips with the fact that her world has changed dramatically. Lily drops out of a school for the blind and stubbornly refuses to believe that she can't make her way around the house. She tries to do too much for herself without really trying to embrace living life as a blind person. Not only do the Girls have to move things around so Lily won't trip and fall, they must also save her—and the house—from a fire she causes on the stovetop.

Dorothy and Blanche implore Rose, who just wants to do everything for her sister, to try to convince Lily to reenroll in the school for the blind so she can begin her journey back to a truly independent life. After six months of trying to do everything for herself, Lily realizes she can't, and asks Rose to move to Chicago to live with her. Though Rose is prepared to join her, Sophia relates the story of how Dorothy refused to coddle her after she suffered her stroke, which, though hard to accept, forced her to do things for herself and accelerated her recovery. Rose decides the only way to help Lily is by helping her help herself.

Whether it's pouring lemonade or placing candlesticks on a table, we want to do things for the people we love, especially when they're suffering. Remember when you do everything for someone, they often learn to do nothing and their independence quickly changes your relationship into one of codependence. When you encourage people to do things they may not feel capable of doing, you allow them to fail and, more importantly, to get back up again.

Party!

ROSE: Blanche, a party is a celebration of life, and it's not just for you, but for your friends who love you.

BLANCHE: No!

ROSE: Stop being so vain. You can't stay "forty-two" forever.

BLANCHE: Yes, you can if you eat right, exercise regularly, and live with women who look a lot older than you.

It's important to remember to celebrate the small things as much as the big things in life. Holidays are, of course, a time when family and friends gather together to enjoy the day, and each other's company. Or, if you're like Rose and Charlie, to conceive a child. Though they enjoyed Christmas, Mother's Day, and Valentine's Day as much as anyone, the Golden Girls never turned down an opportunity to open their home, and their hearts, for a party. Understanding the importance of taking the time to commemorate and enjoy special moments and victories, they've hosted birthdays, weddings and almost weddings, engagement parties, a prison party for Sophia, high school reunions/Trudy McMann memorials, Moonlight Madness soirees, Welcome Back from Rehab, Rose receptions, surprise Congratulations on Your First-Place Essay, Mario bashes, and even a My Husband Is Gone Forever whoop-de-do. In fact, even a visit from a relative, like Sven, is worthy of cake (especially one in the shape of Florida . . . or whatever you can pick up from the Get It While It's Hot Erotic Bake Shop)!

By taking the time to honor happiness, and even sadness, you strengthen your bonds with others, honor your memories, and solidify the foundations of your life.

Your Friends Can Have Friends

BLANCHE: Rose, what was your first impression of me?

ROSE: I thought you wore too much makeup and were a slut. . . . I was wrong. You don't wear too much makeup.

Your friends have other friends, and every so often, you're going to come in contact with them.

The navy may have classified Blanche as a friendly port, but friends of the Girls all knew that the house on Richmond Street was a safe haven for visitors near and far. Classmates and old sweethearts and teachers like Trudy McMann, John Neretti, Malcolm Gordon; work friends Jerry Kennedy and Father Frank Leahy; senior pals including Lillian and Martha; *amici* like Philomena and Dominic Bosco; and even neighbors like Harry, Barbara, and Carol Weston, and even Dreyfuss the dog, were all welcome. While some friends of friends, like Jean, were on their way to becoming friends with benefits, there is also Barbara Thorndyke, Dorothy's new friend, and famed author of such novels as *Evil Wind Over Pensacola*, *So Dark the Waves on Biscayne Bay*, and *Scarlet Dawn at Boca Raton*, who is as difficult to stomach as a literary lunch of a turkey on *Catcher in the Rye* bread and a side of George Bernard slaw. As much as Blanche and Rose try to get along with her, Barbara's condescending, rude, and bigoted behavior proves that she cares more about words than she does people. The Girls understand that everyone has the right to their own friends, but they also believe that it takes a good friend to point out your mistakes. Because they were friends—good friends—Blanche and Rose were willing, for Dorothy's sake, to continue to try to see the good in Barbara. Eventually, Dorothy saw with her own eyes what Blanche and Rose had been trying to tell her and ended her friendship with Barbara.

You're never going to be the only person in someone's life. Since you're not always going to get along with your friend's friends, make the best of it, limit your time with them, and try to see the good your friend sees in them. Unless they're bigots. In that case, just cut them off and keep your friend.

Why Do Men?

ROSE: Why does any man cheat?

DOROTHY: Well, there are two popular theories. One: Men are victims of an evolutionary process which genetically programs their sexual habits.

BLANCHE: What's the other theory?

DOROTHY: Men are scum.

You deserve respect. And a better nickname than "the Big Bug Lady." After being stood up for the third time by Rex Huntington, Blanche is left feeling unattractive, undesirable, and ignored. Worse, she's left at home to spend a lonely night with Dorothy, Rose, and Sophia. While she's willing to forgive Rex for the sake of seeing him in and out of his underwear (which he leaves for her to wash), she begins to wonder whether the term *barrel butt* is a term of endearment. Dorothy believes that Rex's behavior has gone beyond challenging and is starting to really affect Blanche's self-esteem. Speaking from her experience with Michael Tortelli, the captain of her high school football team, Dorothy warns Blanche that despite all of Rex's apologies and excuses, she's in an abusive relationship. Yet it's not until she sees Rex being cruel to Dorothy that she's able to take a step back, acknowledge the kind of man Rex is, and throw him out.

People can sometimes say things they may regret, but it's rare for someone to keep repeating words—or behaviors—by accident. There are too many explanations for why men do . . . anything. Remember that there's no reason or excuse for you to accept being treated with anything less than the kindness, respect, and love you deserve.

Let Go of Anger

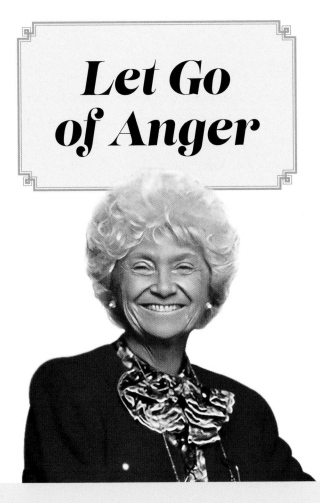

SOPHIA: Anger is a lot like a piece of Shredded Wheat caught under your dentures. If you leave it there, you get a blister and you gotta eat Jell-O all week. If you get rid of it, the sore heals, and you feel better.

DOROTHY: Anger is like a piece of Shredded Wheat?

SOPHIA: You want poetry, you listen to Neil Diamond. You want good advice? You listen to your mother.

Sometimes the only way to move on is to let go.

Dorothy has every right to be angry at Stanley. After thirty-eight years of marriage, she has to hear it from Stanley's lawyer that he is leaving her for Chrissy. Now, after being divorced for two years, they need to come together for their daughter Kate's wedding. Dorothy calls Stanley to invite him, remaining calm all the while by reminding herself that once he is there, he'll be close enough to kill. When the big day comes, Blanche suggests she and Rose stick to Dorothy like a tight shirt on a sweaty farmhand—you know, the type with the big biceps and the hairy chest just glistening in the sun—for moral support (and not, as Blanche's imagination would lead, a morals charge). After Dorothy contemplates stabbing Stanley with the cake knife (after the wedding, so there would be fewer witnesses), she becomes too upset to leave her bedroom. Sophia explains that she should take the opportunity to finally tell Stanley, to his face, just how angry she is. Dorothy takes her advice and explains to Stanley, who for once can't run away, just what happened: how she had to find out from his legal representative that thirty-eight years of sharing and crying and dreaming and fighting and loving and children and diapers and school plays and Little League were over, she begins to feel better.

Whether it's by writing a letter to someone who has passed away, or safely confronting someone who has done you wrong, a sense of closure can help reduce your anger over a situation. Freeing yourself from the anger and resentment that's been weighing you down can allow you to receive, and be open to new, positive relationships.

Treat Your Aging Parents Like Adults

DOROTHY: Honey, can I talk to you as one daughter to another? Do you remember way back when we were teenagers? What was the one thing we wanted most from our mothers?

ROSE: A training bra?

DOROTHY: Honey, the thing we wanted most was to be treated as adults. But then, as we get older, we turn right around and start treating our mothers like little girls.

*T*t can be difficult, if not downright painful, to watch your parents age. (Which is why some children opt to place their parents in Shady Pines Retirement Home, even if it does resemble Sing Sing prison without a movie night.)

Rose is as excited as she is nervous about her mother, Alma, visiting Miami. Though Alma is about the same age as Sophia, Rose views her as much more emotionally and physically frail. She's terrified that Alma is mere moments away from breaking a hip like she did while ice-skating. Alma soon grows sick of being treated like a helpless little girl and decides to leave early. After a heart-to-heart with Dorothy, Rose realizes that though her mother may be advanced in years, she is still healthy and more than capable of living a full and fun life on her own.

Though your parents may need—and want—your help as they age, remember that they deserve to be treated as adults, not infantilized.

Sign Up for Rewards Points

BLANCHE: I need three more people to get the group rate at the hotel.

SOPHIA: I thought hotels always gave you the group rate.

ROSE: Yeah, sweetheart, but this is for the whole night.

apitalism may yield benefits for companies and the executives in the C-suite, but as a consumer, you should benefit for your loyalty to businesses as well.

Though Blanche's reputation precedes her at most of the bars, gas stations, and hospitality establishments in the greater Miami area, she finds herself in a financial jam when organizing a murder-mystery weekend for her museum colleagues at the Queen of the Keys Hotel. As much as she needs Dorothy, Rose, and Sophia to boost attendance to qualify for a group rate, she also needs them to boost her confidence. She wants the weekend to be one her colleagues never forget, mostly so she can position herself to become the new assistant to Kendall Nesbitt, the museum's director of acquisitions. Or any other position he wants her to be in.

Luckily, thanks to Dorothy's sleuthing skills, a good amount of flirting, and her ability to remain within budget even as a suspected murderer, Blanche impresses Kendall enough to remain in the running for the job.

So, whether you're a frequent shopper, a patron of the arts, or have a table on permanent reserve at Don's Crab House, it's important to take advantage of any promotions, coupons, or other marketing initiatives offered by businesses and companies you frequent. And remember, check your local *Pennysaver* (or nowadays your email) for the two-for-one liposuctions offered by Fifi Bolger's husband.

Practice Safe Sex

DOROTHY: Condoms, Rose. Condoms, condoms, condoms!

Anyone who is vibrant, healthy, and sexually active should be practicing safe sex. And, whenever possible, should not be loitering with their friends in a seedy hotel lobby, so as not to be mistaken for a lady of the night.

As the Girls prepare to go on a romantic weekend cruise to the Bahamas with their boyfriends Jeff, Rich, and Randy, Blanche suggests that they take along some protection.

Thanks to modern science and in-store merchandising, the Girls are presented with a wide variety of options. Whether you go for the lambskins or the ultra-sensitives, your purchases are nobody's business but your own. You should not be embarrassed, uncomfortable, or humiliated by shopkeepers or nosy onlookers for making morally and socially responsible decisions.

If, like the Girls, you wind up not having the opportunity to use your protection when and how you'd intended, they need not go to waste. Keep them on hand for future encounters, for friends in need, or to use as water balloons!

Don't Live Afraid

SOPHIA: I said I wasn't scared of dying anymore. I didn't say I was ready to die.

*T*here's nothing to fear but fear itself. That, and the bogeyman.

When she chokes and falls unconscious, Sophia finds herself standing before a bright white light and hearing a familiar voice . . . James Cagney. It isn't actually Cagney, of course, but rather her dearly departed husband, Sal, doing his famed impersonation. She's thrilled to see him, and eager to restart their relationship, which she once described as being like the veal Parmesan she fixed him after one of their fights. The veal was tough and stubborn like him, the tomato sauce was hot and spicy like Sophia, and the mozzarella cheese was like their love: It stretches, but it never breaks.

After Rose revives her, Sophia seems to be a new, seemingly fearless, woman. She starts taking more and more risks, driving, and even jumping into a hay-stack from a second-story window. Dorothy beings to worry about her mother's reckless behavior. Things settle down when Sophia explains that her near-death experience allowed her to realize that instead of living in fear of the future she needed to live for the day. Every moment can be precious and—if you add life's most flavorful ingredient, *love*—between partners, children, or friends, you'll be able to stretch it out like mozzarella cheese on veal Parmesan.

Some relationships only last until checkout time. Or, until they reveal they're the Cheeseman, or they quit their job as a lawyer and become a clown. Other relationships can last decades, even after one party dies. Being overly fearful of the end of a relationship—or the outcome of any experience—will do nothing but keep you from enjoying the start of something new or, worse, everything that comes after.

Life's Tough

ROSE: Sometimes, life just isn't fair, kiddo.

There are toys, and then there are treasured family heirlooms like Rose's teddy bear, Fernando. As her constant companion since she was six years old, Fernando is filled with more than love, he is filled with love and life. But when Blanche accidentally gifts him to Daisy, a Sunshine Cadet who decides to hold him ransom, the Girls fear they'll never see Fernando again. Blanche and Dorothy try to reason with her, reminding her that Sunshine Cadets are taught all about honesty, decency, and respect for one's elders; Daisy reminds them that Sunshine Cadets also teach the need to pay for your mistakes. And this one will cost them.

Caught between a rock and a hard place, and Rose's directive to *get the damn teddy bear back,* Blanche agrees to pay Daisy for Fernando's return. However, Rose stops Blanche before she can get her checkbook. She's been doing a lot of thinking, and she'll just have to accept that, after all their years of love and companionship, she and Fernando are meant to part company. "From time to time," she explains, "life deals everyone an unfriendly hand. There's nothing you can do but learn from such things." Surprisingly, the lesson to be learned, in this particular case, is *not* to just roll over and accept every injustice; it's to snatch your bear from the arms of a too-slow Sunshine Cadet, slam the door in her face, and move on with your life, best friends beside you.

Part of growing up is learning to deal with loss and disappointment. Rather than accepting the things you can't change, try to change the things you can't accept, and slam the door on anyone who wants to extort you for your childhood possessions.

Parties Take Planning

BLANCHE: Dorothy, would you please check my list and see if I forgot to invite anybody to my Moonlight Madness party?

DOROTHY: Sure. The women.

BLANCHE: Pardon me?

DOROTHY: The women. You invited twelve men and no women.

*P*arties cannot be thrown together at the last minute. You need to carefully consider the guest list, menu, activities, and how, exactly, you're going to get your guests to either leave or . . . spend the night.

After checking Blanche's list of invitees to her Moonlight Madness party, Dorothy worries that all the male guests will be bored, what with only one Blanche to go around for all of them. Blanche, for her part, isn't worried because she's planned everything perfectly: There's a full moon, a time when men's passions, like the tides, are pulled to their highest achingly unbearable peak. But just in case the moon's not enough to do all that, she's also filling a watermelon with tequila.

Unfortunately, the evening doesn't go exactly as planned. Though she took great pains with the guest list, rather than turning out to be one of the most romantic evenings of Blanche's life, the men seem to only be paying attention to Dorothy, Rose, and Sophia—and even their neighbor Carol. Thanks to careful party planning, and the power of a leap year's full moon, each guest has a memorable time—even if the focus of Blanche's affection shifts *his* focus from Blanche to her easily stolen jewelry.

The key to any successful soiree, whether it's on the lanai, in the living room, starting at the doormat outside your door, or at the foot of your bed, is to take the needs, wants, and desires of your guests to heart. Unless all they want to do is to steal your jewelry, in which case you should invite the police over.

We're All in This Together

DOROTHY: Sure, you're five years older. So am I, so is Blanche. All right, so you have a few more wrinkles. So do I, so does Blanche. All right, you're a little thicker around the middle. So is Blanche.

*F*riends share more than just cheesecake. They share experiences, setbacks, joys, and, naturally, the issues that come with growing up, and older. Just don't try to share their electric blanket when you're both sick.

When the grief-counseling center closes, Rose is overwhelmed with the prospect of finding a new job and puts off the search for as long as she can. She's terrified that she's become old and useless and there's nothing anyone—not even the Girls—can do to make her young again. It's up to Dorothy to remind her that she and Blanche are in the same rocky and, when it comes to Blanche, wide boat.

When you feel like you're all alone, when no one else could ever truly understand your situation, try reaching out to your friends. You'll find more often than not that they're not only sympathetic to your problem, but have probably gone through something similar themselves.

There Is No Road Map to Quality Time

SOPHIA: Quality time has to come naturally. It happens when you're not thinking about it.

Though you may be able to force an ailing dancing partner to samba all night in exchange for a night to remember, it's impossible to force a truly meaningful memory to happen.

After returning from yet another funeral, Dorothy worries that though they live under the same roof the time she and Sophia spend together isn't necessarily quality time. She vows to make the most of the time they have left and offers to take Sophia wherever she wants to go for the weekend. Though Sophia suspects Dorothy may be setting her up for a return visit to Shady Pines, they wind up at Disney World, a place she's been asking to visit for years. Sophia wants to make new memories and ride on Space Mountain, Dorothy prefers to stay in their hotel room and reminisce over old memories.

When Dorothy finds Sophia in the hotel bar, she comes to understand two things: (1) Some lounge singers really know their way round a chorus of "It's a Small World," and (2) like the lightning bugs Sophia used to catch in Sicily and store in airtight jars, you can't capture magical moments forever. Before they leave, Dorothy gives Sophia the magic moment she wanted—a ride on Space Mountain.

Remember that it's the moments in between the big, manufactured memories, the naturally occurring ones, like a shared conversation over a game of cards, that can prove to be the most meaningful.

No Family Is Perfect

BLANCHE: You know, my family had a few dollars, and I loved them dearly, but when you get right down to it, basically, they were trash.

The family you have may not necessarily be the family you want—or think you want. Even if you charge them rent.

Like us, none of the Girls come from a perfect family. Adopted at age eight by kindly farmers into a family that gave her nine siblings and countless relatives and chores, Rose always longed to meet her biological parents. When she finally had the opportunity to meet her father, she learned that he was not, as she'd hoped, Bob Hope, but instead was a monk.

Rather than be forced into a marriage by her traditional Sicilian family, Sophia left them all to start a new life in America. Though she maintained a good relationship with her brother Angelo, who pretended to be a priest, the bond she shared with her sister Angela was marred by years of misunderstandings and resentments.

The Hollingsworth children—Blanche, Charmaine, Virginia, and Clay—all proved equally irresistible to men and drove their parents, Big Daddy and Big Mommy, to distraction. Later, Blanche had to contend not only with the revelation of Big Daddy's affair, but his marriage to a much younger woman and, worst of all, the knowledge that her proud Southern Baptist family had roots in the Jewish corners of Buffalo, New York.

And though the trajectory of Dorothy's life was directed, at least in part, by her immigrant parents' drive for her to do better than they could, it was equally influenced by her close bond with her brother, Phil, with whom she often shared outfits, and with her sister, Gloria, whose financial success served as a constant reminder of Dorothy's financial struggles.

Though none of the Girls' families were able to provide the Girls with everything they needed or wanted emotionally or materially, each knew that they needed to at least interact with and accept their families—for better or worse—on their own terms. They took whatever love and support they could, and, when necessary, separated from, or came to terms with, their toxic relatives and relationships.

Every family has its share of comedy and drama. It's up to you whether you want to keep tuning in for it.

Emotions Are Complicated

DOROTHY: I was feeling jealous and lonely, and God knows what else.

BLANCHE: Magenta . . . that's what I call it when I get that way. All kinds of feelings tumbling all over themselves. Well, you know you're not quite blue because you're not really sad, and although you're a little bit jealous, you wouldn't say you're green with envy, and every now and then you realize you're kind of scared but you'd hardly call yourself yellow.

Much like Blanche's choice of funeral or wedding attire, the world isn't black or white. It's filled with an infinite variety of colors—including whatever Rose's original hair shade is—colors that inform and influence people's perceptions, actions, and reactions. Similarly, our emotions are rarely just one thing, especially when they concern unresolved issues or relationships.

When Dorothy is hesitant to cancel her date with Jeffrey the commodore, she convinces Blanche to spend time with Stanley the depressed. Blanche reluctantly agrees to the plan and is surprised when she finds herself enjoying spending time with Dorothy's ex. Though Dorothy is initially supportive of their new friendship, things take a decidedly complicated turn when Jeffrey dumps her. Old resentments and jealousies bubble up to the surface, and Dorothy is left to confront how and why she's feeling what she's feeling.

A friend understands that sometimes what appears to be anger is actually a cover for a complicated and layered set of emotions. A good friend is one who is willing to help unravel the threads, one by one, until you feel better.

Sometimes You Just Have to Let Them Talk

ROSE: In St. Olaf, the mother was always with the daughter when she gave birth. And if the mother was out of town, then the mother of the father was there. And if she was out of town, then we'd call Lucky Gunther.

DOROTHY: Oh, what the hell. She has a birthday coming up. Why, Rose?

*T*alking through a problem, or just talking about nothing, could be just what your friend needs.

Rose has a St. Olaf story for every occasion. Yet not every occasion warrants a St. Olaf story. I mean, there are just so many hours in the day. Aside from trying to ease tensions between Rebecca and her mother, Blanche, there's little the Girls can do when she comes back to Miami to deliver her baby. So Rose offers to do what she does best: tell a St. Olaf story. Though no one is ready to hear it, Dorothy understands that, in stressful times, it sometimes helps to just get something off your chest, to at least try to contribute something. So Rose tells the story about how, in St. Olaf, when no family is around to help a woman at the time of her delivery, they call Lucky Gunther. You see, after the thresher accident, they replaced Lucky's arm with a forceps. Yep. Lucky Gunther. He was in charge of delivering babies and handing out corn at the Rotary picnics.

Helpful? Not really. But it certainly passed the time and got everyone thinking about something other than their *own* baby drama.

Sometimes people just need to talk to fill the silence, fill the time, or distract themselves, and others, from a stressful situation. Let them talk. And if they go on for too long, just tell them to shut up, Rose.

Live by a Code of Ethics

BLANCHE: Blanche Devereaux never goes out with another woman's husband. Oh, except for that one time. Now, that was not my fault. She was pronounced dead. Those paramedics never give up.

*I*t's important to hold yourself to a standard. Even if those standards don't include wearing underwear.

After thirty-eight years of living with, and being cheated on, by Stanley, Dorothy understands how devastating adultery can be on everyone. But she finds herself in a difficult position when she discovers that Glen, the gym teacher she's been seeing, is married. Blanche believes if they're realistic and discreet, they could continue seeing each other. Life, she opines, doesn't always work out the way you want it to, so you need to grab happiness where you can get it. Rose and Sophia take a decidedly different point of view and think she should end the affair. Though Dorothy thinks she can handle checking in and out of hotel rooms and discreetly taking separate cars, she soon realizes that she's not cut out to be the other woman. Their love just isn't enough, and if she stays, she's throwing away her future happiness.

By knowing who you are and what lines you will or won't cross, you'll be in a better position to point your chin(s) up, thrust your breasts forward, and thrive.

Say "I Love You"

DOROTHY: I never really told him I loved him, so I want to make sure I tell you.

SOPHIA: Oh, pussycat. "Dear Ma. Thanks for giving me life and thanks for making it good. I love you." And I love you, too, pussycat.

DOROTHY: And I love you, too. And I'm glad you're my mom.

SOPHIA: And I'm glad you're my baby.

*L*ife moves fast. Sometimes faster than you can say, "Bacon, lettuce, and potato." You must find the time to tell people how you feel about them.

Though Dorothy can remember many wonderful moments with her father, Sal, she feels their relationship lacks a sense of closure. There are just too many things she's never gotten to say to him, including goodbye. She sets out to get all her stored-up emotions out in a letter to him. When Dorothy finally finishes the letter and gets everything—all the little hurts as well as all the good memories—onto the page, she not only realizes that Sal was a pretty good father, but that she doesn't want to feel the same lack of completion in her relationship with Sophia. She writes her mother a letter of her own and gives them both the gift of communication, honesty, and connection.

Telling your friends and family that you love them is sometimes easier said than done. It can be awkward, or scary, to tell people that you love them. Even if you may both know how you feel, saying it out loud, writing it, or even texting it—before it's too late—will allow you both to *feel* your connection more completely.

Attitude Is Everything

SOPHIA: I remember what your cousin Frederico used to say: "People waste their time pondering whether a glass is half-empty or half-full. Me, I just drink whatever's in the glass."

DOROTHY: Ma, Cousin Frederico was a hopeless alcoholic who played boccie ball with an imaginary friend named Little Luigi.

ositive steps can lead to positive results. And retelling the tales of positive role models like "Gus and the Recliner," "Gunilla Gets a Catalog," and "Ilsa, the Girl Who Could Make Bad Food Good" can lead to being hit on the head with a newspaper.

Thanks to the "Create Your Own Happiness" seminars she's been attending, Rose feels terrific. In fact, she feels like life is a giant weenie roast and she's the biggest weenie. She convinces the Girls to join her, but Dorothy's negativity casts serious doubts on the seminar's benefits. Later, much to her surprise, things take a decidedly positive turn once Dorothy starts approaching things with a more open and optimistic attitude. If she can finally get a good cut of roast beef from the nasty four-fingered butcher, maybe things really can improve for her and she'll be able to get a guy who is honest, caring, and with eyes only for her. Yet despite her best efforts, things remain lousy. Sometimes, some good luncheon meat is all you can expect out of life.

Though a positive, optimistic attitude can provide a way to get past trivial inconveniences, you must remember to always accept life on its own terms, and keep in mind that miracles, much like the ending of a St. Olaf story, may never happen.

Let Your Children Live Their Own Lives

ROSE: In the animal kingdom, the whole idea is to teach offspring to fend for themselves. Humans are the only ones who think it's their duty to care for children their entire lives.

DOROTHY: You know, Rose, sometimes you really say some wise things.

ROSE: We're also the only species who use corn holders that look like corn on the cob when we eat corn on the cob.

DOROTHY: Oops! Spoke too soon.

The point of raising your children is to teach them to be self-sufficient. And to give you grandchildren. Like many people with grown children, the Golden Girls were no strangers to wanting to interfere in the lives of their grown children. Rose's children Kirsten, Bridget, Gunilla, Adam, and Charlie Jr. were the apples of that farm girl's eye. Dorothy felt she needed to object when her son, Michael, wanted to marry the much older Lorraine, and she and Rose needed to intervene in his affair with Rose's daughter, Bridget. Blanche was distant from her children, especially sons Biff, Doug, and Skippy, and daughter Janet, perhaps, at least in part, because she allowed her children to be raised by a succession of nannies. Old and new tensions arose when her daughter Rebecca came to town. After the two didn't see each other for years, Blanche struggles to put aside her criticism of Rebecca's weight gain to help her extricate herself from her relationship with her abusive fiancé, Jeremy. Later, Blanche has great difficulty accepting Rebecca's decision to be artificially inseminated.

Of course, no mother was as involved in her children's lives as Sophia. Though she was as proud of Gloria as she was confused by Phil, her direct and constant contact with Dorothy allowed for almost a decade more of parental interference. Proud to have been playing with Dorothy's head for over sixty years about things such as Santa Claus, the Easter Bunny, and her IQ, Sophia never hesitated to go behind Dorothy's back to get her a date via a matchmaker; a better rate on the flowers, catering, and janitorial services for a banquet; or even to just get her out of the house. Regardless of the level of manipulation, each of the four mothers did what they did out of love.

It's hard not to interfere with your children's life, so try remember that you raised them to be self-sufficient people. Your children's happiness, health, and safety were—and remain—your main concern, you must allow them to make their own decisions and be who they are.

Tell a Story

BLANCHE: Well, like any good story, mine was deliberately ambiguous, thus affording the listener the opportunity to glean from it whatever he may. Besides, I just hate it when I'm left out of conversations.

Storytelling is a great way to share experiences, offer advice, and help people make their own decisions. Other times it's a tool for pure entertainment.

All four of the Golden Girls know their way around a story. Except for Rose, who knows her way up the stairs and down the stairs and up the stairs and down the stairs of each and every inch of a St. Olaf tale. At best, her tales of idiocy convince the Girls to leave their doubts and confusion behind. At worst, her meandering anecdotes of the town founded by Heinrich von Anderdonnen, the man who came up with the idea to can tuna in its own juices, motivate them to leave the room.

Blanche plays fast and loose with the truth; no surprise there. Though she tells many, *many* contradictory tales of her romantic deflowering, all her stories about her life and times in the deep and slutty—er, *sultry* South—offered an unmistakable, if somewhat narcissistic, viewpoint that provides listeners with a clear perspective of the situation.

Dorothy's stories, often retellings of one of her many past defeats, serve as lessons in humility, self-reliance, resiliency, and, in the case of Stan, abject disappointment, coming with a practical, actionable, and usually less-than-positive worldview.

Of course, all of Sophia's detailed and vivid depictions of her life in Sicily indicate she doesn't stick to the truth (or even steer a horse and buggy close to it). Because she knows that old-world wisdom is made more palatable with a healthy topping of Italian cheese, her stories make extravagant claims about knowing Golda Meir (or at least her husband, Oscar Mayer), being on a game show with Mussolini as the host, and claiming to have been wooed by notable figures including Winston Churchill, Sigmund Freud, and Pablo Picasso.

Before writing became universal, human history was passed down through the spoken word. But thanks to modern technology, we've been able to share our stories and experiences through television shows, books, movies, and, if you're lucky, on someone's windshield using the heel of your Pappagallo pump. For your own good, and the good of humanity, share your stories!

Use Metaphors

DOROTHY: Uh, let's say that you make Miles a batch of your delicious creamy cupcakes. And he loves them so much that he wants you to make them all the time . . . But let's say that even though he loves your cupcakes more than life itself, one day he decides to try somebody else's cupcakes. For lack of a better example, let's say, my cupcakes. And I, in a mad, passionate moment, uh, forget myself and let him try my cupcakes.

ROSE: No offense, Dorothy, but your cupcakes are dry and tasteless. Nobody ever likes your cupcakes.

DOROTHY: My cupcakes are moist and delicious. Men love my cupcakes.

Some things are hard to say. And some things are even harder to understand. Especially if you're trying to explain it in a roundabout way to a Swedish meatball.

Blanche's Moonlight Madness party descends into a moment of temporary madness when Dorothy and Miles, Rose's boyfriend, share a passionate kiss on the lanai. Well, they kiss on the lips while *standing* on the lanai. Racked with guilt, Dorothy feels the need to confess to Rose. In an effort to test the waters before diving into the unvarnished truth of what happened, Dorothy tries to use a metaphor to see how Rose would feel if Miles strayed from his normal dessert in favor of something with a little more . . . flavor. Of course, the metaphor goes over Rose's head, but the point does eventually get made.

Metaphors are fantastic linguistic tools for you to introduce difficult topics of conversation gently and respectfully, especially to people you care about. However, try using metaphors that your friends can easily understand or relate to. If they don't quite get what you're saying, feel free to invite your mother into the conversation to bluntly state your case.

Take It One Step at a Time

ROSE: I'll never be cured, but I know now I can live without drugs my whole life, one day at a time.

SOPHIA: I'm just glad you got that monkey off your back.

ROSE: I never had a monkey on my back, Sophia. Although, when I was a child, I had a chicken named Gordon. And he was a great singer, too. Gordon could cluck the scores of all the big Broadway musicals.

*L*ike many other illnesses, addiction should not be considered a shameful or embarrassing ailment. It can be treated, but it's up to you to take the first steps toward your own recovery. You can even start with teeny steps—remember, you're a person moving toward recovery, not Godzilla attacking a city.

After Sophia knocks Rose's prescription pills down the drain the day before a holiday, the Girls realize Rose will have to wait longer than expected to get a refill. Rose soon becomes uncharacteristically aggressive. It's only when she's back on her pills, and calm, that Rose explains that's she's been taking the medication since wrenching her back in a farming accident thirty years ago.

The Girls think Rose has grown dependent on the pills. But to prove she can quit whenever she wants to, Rose gives them to Dorothy. Later, the Girls find Rose "rearranging the cabinets" in the middle of the night. Rose is too embarrassed to seek professional help at a rehabilitation center and thinks she can simply quit cold turkey. Though the Girls have their doubts, they reluctantly agree to do whatever it takes: stories, Bundt cake, chin-ups, or even a spirited game of Googenspritzer to help get her through the night. Despite their support, Rose realizes that she can neither overcome her addiction alone nor can she rely on her friends to help her 24/7. She knows that in order to take the steps toward recovery, she must takes the steps toward the phone to call for professional help.

It can be difficult to admit, first to yourself, and then to others, that you have a problem. Rather than framing addiction as a shameful defect in your personality or moral fiber, try seeing it as any other disease that must be dealt with in a concerted, consistent manner. Once you do, you can then commit to your own recovery by finding a support system that works for you.

Ask for Forgiveness

BLANCHE: Rose, honey, there's something I have to say to you. It's just two little words but they are the hardest two little words in all the whole world for me to say.

ROSE: "Not tonight"?

*T*hough few actions compare to Rose putting sunscreen on a chicken so it won't burn in the oven, everyone makes mistakes.

Blanche cannot understand why her newly single brother, Clayton, can't find a woman to settle down with. She sets him up on a date, but it ends early, and he bumps into Rose. Clayton explains to her that it's not the quality of the women that's the problem, it's that they're women. Though Rose encourages Clayton to tell Blanche that he's gay, he throws Rose under the bus and says that he and Rose slept together. Blanche, in turn, throws a fit. The truth eventually comes out, and Blanche must find a way to repair her relationship with both her brother and with Rose.

It's easy for a relationship, even a long-standing or deeply meaningful one, to get stuck, or even end, because of a mistake or a miscommunication. The only way for anyone to move on, even tentatively, is to acknowledge the mistake, ask for forgiveness, and do the work to try to do better in the future.

Don't Let a Man Break Up Your Friendship

SOPHIA: Let me tell you a story. Sicily, 1912. Picture this: Two young girls, best friends, who shared three things: a pizza recipe, some dough, and a dream. Everything is going great until one day, a fast-talking pepperoni salesman gallops into town. Of course, both girls are impressed. He dates one one night, the other the next night. Pretty soon, he drives a wedge between them. Before you know it, the pizza suffers, the business suffers, the friendship suffers. The girls part company and head for America, never to see one another again. Rose, one of those girls was me. The other one you probably know as Mama Celeste.

You're going to share some interests with your friends, like pizza toppings, Elvis Presley, or freezing your heads after your deaths. But sometimes, that interest is going to be a man.

At several points in *The Golden Girls* run, two or more of the Girls find themselves interested in the same man. Both Blanche and Sophia went nuts for Fidel Santiago, while Dorothy, Blanche, and Rose all posed for, and sought the attention of, the very artistic, very gay Laszlo. It was inevitable that at least one man would try to have it both ways (or twice in one night), like that two-timing Elliot did when he made a pass at Blanche while dating Dorothy, or when Stan tried, literally and figuratively, to come between Dorothy and her sister, Gloria.

But throughout the years, the Girls understood that though men may come and go (and, according to the screeching sounds emanating from Blanche's bedroom, they go quite happily), it is friendship that remains.

Everyone Has Their Own Idea of Fun

MR. HA HA: Well, it says here on my Ha Ha birthday list that Bobby is seven, Jeannie is nine, and Dorothy is . . .

DOROTHY: I'll punch your heart out, Ha Ha.

*W*hether it's crashing someone else's high school reunion, donning the back end of a horse costume, or eating brussels sprouts, your friends may not enjoy everything you do.

When Rose plans a fun surprise birthday party at Mr. Ha Ha's Hot Dog Hacienda, it's unfortunate that the party is not for a child, but for Dorothy. Though she's always complained that her birthday parties were dull and boring, Dorothy still can't get into the spirit of things that the other birthday boys and girls seem to be enjoying. To make Rose feel better, she and Blanche try to have fun with their foot-long Mr. Ha Ha Dogs and drinking their thirty-two-ounce Cherry Burpees—especially since drinking three of these drinks will allow them to keep Mr. Ha Ha's hat. Yet despite their fun and singing, things go a little off-key when Dorothy is called up onstage by none other than Mr. Ha Ha himself for the Mr. Ha Ha Birthday Roundup. Though Dorothy begrudgingly joins the other birthday girls and boys onstage, it's clear from the look on her face, and her verbal threats to Mr. Ha Ha's physical safety, that she's not having as much fun as Rose had hoped she would.

Though you and your friends may share lots of interests, you each have your own likes and dislikes. So, when planning activities, especially those in honor or celebration of someone's special day or achievements, try to take their interests into account.

There Are Friends, and Then There Are Friends

STEPHANIE: Look, Rose, we all go our separate ways around here. Besides, you have your own friends, don't you?

Roommates may be wanted, but friends are needed.

Things get muddled, well, even more muddled for Rose, when she overextends herself and suffers an esophageal spasm that lands her in the hospital. Thinking she died, she reevaluates her life and determines to become "Rose Nylund, the girl who is going to eat life!" She starts spending her days—and especially her nights—with a new group of beach friends, that leads to the unexpected result of the entire household's sleeping cycles getting thrown out of whack. Dorothy and Blanche grow concerned about Rose's new lifestyle, but she refuses to calm down and curtail her new antics with her new friends, even going so far as to move into a beachside apartment with two new roommates.

As much as Blanche and Dorothy miss having her around the Richmond Street house, things prove tougher on Rose. She loses touch with her beach pals and misses having friends, roommates—or *anyone*—in the room while she's talking. Rose realizes that her new living arrangement is quite different than what she's used to and that there's a huge difference between roommates and friends. She returns home—to her friends. And because they're her friends, Dorothy and Blanche quickly get out the bowls and ice cream to get her up to speed on what she's missed.

Not all friends are roommates, and not all roommates are friends. If you're lucky enough to share your home with the people you share your life with, remember to take the time to celebrate and honor them, and your relationship. But don't be too loud, or the Schmaltz Police will come knocking.

Make Your Expectations Clear

BLANCHE: Now, let me clear up any confusion you might have. I don't want to be treated as your equal.

JERRY: You don't?

BLANCHE: I want to be treated a lot better than you. I mean, really. Like a goddess who likes to go bar hopping.

I t can be difficult to start a new relationship without knowing, and explaining, what you're looking for. Even if you're just looking through the obituaries to see who you've outlived.

Dorothy has a blind date but also a chance to go to *Beatlemania*, a show that means a lot to her given that she missed her chance to see the Beatles when they played Shea Stadium in the 1960s. Seemingly not remembering the trouble she got into in Season 1 when she went out with Stan in Dorothy's place, Blanche agrees to fill in on the date and is smitten when Jerry, a handsome widower shows up. Dorothy has a great time transferring her lust for George Harrison onto (and under) Don, the musician who plays George (and understudies for Paul) in the show. Unfortunately, Blanche's date goes poorly. Blanche is surprised Jerry made her split the check and didn't hold the door for her. Even worse: She woke up alone. The outrage!

Jerry later explains that since his wife died he's been reading up on modern women and thought he understood what they wanted, but really he's simply confused. For once, Blanche enters a sex drought and Dorothy enjoys a lot of . . . *rain*. Dorothy's bumper crop is short-lived, however, when she's unable to lower her expectations and standards and accept what a truly awful musician Don is when not singing in a Liverpudlian accent. Blanche and Jerry, on the other hand, talk about, and try to meet, each other's standards and expectations.

Take the time before starting a new relationship, or even a friendship, to understand what you're looking for. Once you appreciate and understand what you can and cannot compromise on, you'll be in a better position to get what you want. (Even if that position is beneath a mirror hung over the bed.)

Go to Therapy

DOROTHY: Dr. Halperin is really working wonders with Stan. You know, he's gotten him to transfer his love for me to a fake monkey.

BLANCHE: Why not use a fake woman?

DOROTHY: Oh, well, honey, that's why Stan went to the psychiatrist in the first place.

Friends can be wonderful sounding boards when you need a late-night cheesecake to deal with life's ebbs and flows. But sometimes, like when dealing with an ex-husband who can't let go, a sister who pushes your buttons, or jealousy over a traffic-cone-shaped fake monkey, a trained therapist can help you really work through your issues.

Stan's issues regarding . . . well, *everything*, but mostly his attachment to Dorothy, have made him a needy shell of a man. Realizing that he needs professional help, he seeks the expertise of psychiatrist, and author of *Monkey Love*, Dr. Halperin, who provides him with tools, including Fifi the fake monkey, to become an independent and happy man. Finally confident in his ability to separate, he thanks Dorothy for thirty-eight years of love, friendship, and memories. Dorothy is too stunned to say ciao to him in the doctor's office, but later she's even more surprised to see him—off the monkey and on her sister, Gloria. (Which is why therapy is best when it's an ongoing practice.)

Not everyone has access to famous psychotherapists, like St. Olaf's Sigmund and Roy Freud, who you may know from their bestseller *If I Have All the Cheese I Want, Why Am I Still Unhappy?* However, there are good people everywhere who are trained to help you with everything from dealing with your mother to living with your roommates to aging. And if you find a real quack? Remember that there are plenty of highly skilled pepperoni in the sea.

Give Back

SOPHIA: The winner of this year's Volunteer Vanguard Award is . . . Rose.

ROSE: Yes!

SOPHIA: Hand me that glass of water, please. Wow! What a surprise! Ladies and gentlemen, for the first time in history, we have a posthumous winner, Agnes Bradshaw!

ROSE: It's a fix! She's dead! She doesn't need that on her mantel. She's on her mantel!

ith the possible exception of winning the Shady Pines Mother-Daughter Beauty Pageant or a giveaway for a free prostate exam, there are few things more rewarding than being of service to others. All the Golden Girls spent their time volunteering for worthy causes. Blanche is able to collect signatures and phone numbers from innumerable men while soliciting support for various political and social campaigns. Sophia's time as a candy striper may have gone unnoticed by the Girls, but her patients certainly appreciated her efforts, as did Father Rossi, to whom she donated canned goods. Dorothy helped raise awareness for the wetlands and various other causes. No one volunteered more than Rose, though. She protested with the Friends of the Sea Mammals to draw attention to the way dolphins were treated, canvassed to save the tree on Mrs. Claxton's property, signed up for raffles and bake sales, joined Blanche in volunteering as a Big Sister, and even sent in a contribution to Save the Rich. Even with their donating to rummage sales, babysitting neighborhood children, and serving at a soup kitchen, their biggest gift, at least monetarily, might be when they donated their winning lottery ticket to the homeless shelter.

Though it's important to give back, you do need to pace yourself. At one point, Rose drives herself to collapse when, in addition to offering to bake Joanie Winston's wedding cake, she commits to addressing three thousand envelopes, picking up the decorations for the church's hootenanny, washing cars, and giving blood before 7:00 p.m. And though Blanche's granddaddy always said, "Idle hands are the devil's workshop," he also said, "Sitting on concrete will give you hemorrhoids." Which is to say that as important as it is to pick and choose your anecdotes, it's equally important to learn how to say no and avoid overextending—and exhausting—yourself.

Donating your time and energy toward causes you believe in allows you the chance to enrich the lives of those directly benefiting from your efforts. In turn, you're sure to feel a great sense of accomplishment, pride, and humility knowing that you've made a difference in the world.

You Don't Need Plastic Surgery

BLANCHE: I look at my face all the time. How different could it be leaning over? . . . Oh my God! Oh my God, Dorothy, why didn't you tell me about this before?

DOROTHY: Only on your back, Blanche. That way everything slides back and you look like you just had a face-lift.

BLANCHE: Oh, you're right. I'm gorgeous. I'm gonna have to meet men lying down.

SOPHIA: I thought you did.

DOROTHY: Of course that way, not only does your face fall back, but your chest does, too. Unfortunately, it falls back and off to the side.

As long as you're doing it for you, in moderation, and under the supervision of trained and trusted medical professionals, there's nothing wrong with a nip or tuck or other procedure to help you look like Cindy Lou Peeples, Susan Armstrong, Kim Fung-Toi, or even Myron Zucker.

Blanche has always been fashion-forward, so it's a good thing that breasts are back in fashion! And though she may sometimes feel the need to enhance them with an air-filled support bra to get a part in a play, she herself has described them as "perfect champagne glass-sized orbs of dancing loveliness." When she gets a big bonus check from work, she's thrilled with the prospect of hiring Dr. Myron Rosensweig, the Picasso of plastic surgeons, to give her what God didn't. Dorothy supports her decision, as long as he doesn't attach a new breast to her forehead. While Rose thinks plastic surgery is too drastic to ever be considered, Dorothy admits to having had her eyes done years before. Though the Girls entertain the idea of surgery, they know that it isn't for everyone. There are lots of ways you can look younger without undergoing a medical procedure. Clever positioning of lighting, mirrors, or even your own body can smooth out wrinkles, perk up your assets, or just distract people from the areas you think are problematic.

Feel free to avail yourself of cosmetic surgery if you think it will help you feel better about yourself. Don't feel pressured to undergo the risk of a surgical procedure to live up to someone's idea of what beauty is. After all, you are golden just the way you are.

You Are Your Own Best Advocate

ROSE: You can't write me off just because I'm not thirtysomething. I have experience. And wisdom. And insight. I'd be perfect for this job. You see, I am the battered consumer. I drive a Gremlin, for God's sake.

*F*inding a job requires, at the very least, a momentary suspension of humility and a few exaggerations of your prior experience. Just be sure to add "double-jointed" under the Special Skills section of your résumé and not under Education.

When Charlie's pension is cut off, Rose finds herself in need of more money. Since her job at the counseling center doesn't pay enough to cover the bills, she needs to find a new one. After she's turned down for a job at a pet store because she's seen as too old, Dorothy and Blanche urge her to reach out to Enrique Mas, the local consumer affairs reporter on TV, about the age discrimination she's facing. When she visits the television station and discovers Enrique is hiring a production assistant, Rose asks if she can apply, but Enrique tells her she is too old. Incensed and frustrated that, once again, she's being judged on her age and not abilities, Rose gives an impassioned speech that convinces Enrique to at least give her a chance to prove she would be a valuable asset to the station. With the Girls' help, Rose tests hair-removal products, writes up an accurate report, and gets the job.

Your résumé can only do so much heavy lifting (even if you mention heavy lifting as a skill). You need to show your prospective employer that you are the right person for the job you want, and the only person they should want for the job they're offering.

Take Time to Heal

SOPHIA: I said it before, and I'll say it again. Sluts just heal quicker.

You can never truly know how long it will take someone to recover from a physical, mental, or emotional injury, especially if it's been suffered over a long period of time . . . or if that person is trying to bilk the insurance company.

Though it would take less time if he went around her, Stanley finally admits that he needs help getting over Dorothy. After the divorce that ended their thirty-eight-years-long first marriage and the prenup that derailed their second one before she even walked down the aisle, Dorothy is anxious to be rid of Stanley once and for all, so she agrees to attend his therapy sessions with him if doing so will help that happen. While in session, they all come to realize that Stan's obsession with Dorothy may actually be an obsession with Sophia, whom Stan sees as a replacement for his own mother, who died before they could resolve their relationship. Though Dorothy wants to do what she can to hasten a permanent separation from Stan, both she and Sophia understand that he, like anyone, needs time to heal from decades of trauma.

Meanwhile, Blanche's new relationship with Jerry Kennedy isn't newsworthy because of his status as Miami's most eligible newscaster, but because of his own damaged relationship with his still-very-much-alive, and domineering, mother. In the end, Blanche's weeks of emotional and—since it's Blanche—*acrobatically physical investment* is for naught as she loses Jerry to a previous girlfriend. Luckily, some injuries are just superficial, and Blanche bounces back in just a few minutes.

Getting over a breakup or hardship can often take longer, or shorter, than expected, so give yourself and others some grace and try not to rush through the process.

Encourage Others

BLANCHE: Now, look, you have to discover the sensuality of baseball. There're just many, many, many similarities between baseball and makin' love. The mental preparation, the rush of adrenaline, the unspecified duration of the game.

SOPHIA: And you should hear the cheers coming from Blanche's room on Old-Timers' Day.

*R*ather than encouraging someone to place their hopes for the future on a bald pinhead with the morals of a maggot who makes his living selling plastic dog doo (aka Stan), try helping them reach their own full potential.

Blanche has been dating professional baseball player Stevie since he found her number written on the dugout wall. He has, as the graffiti promised, been having a good time, but Blanche thinks she can help him professionally, too. Though she can't coach him on the finer points of the game, she can encourage him and give him a shot of self-esteem. For Blanche knows that though some people are great artists or musicians, everyone has a talent, and hers is molding men. To that end, she instructs Stevie to wear lingerie under his uniform. She believes it'll help his game—and she's right. His batting average skyrockets to over .300, even though he does, occasionally, tear his camisole while swinging the bat. In fact, he's so improved that he's been offered a position with a team in Japan. Though Blanche is sad to not share any locker-room showers with him, she remembers that she offered to help Stevie for his own good, and for the good of the baseball fans who expect something of her. Though any man can tell you that she is very, *very* good.

The hard part about encouraging someone to spread their wings is knowing, eventually, they'll fly away. As a friend, a teacher, or even a parent, you must try to remember that it's partly because of you that the person you help is able to pursue their own goals and successes. And *that* is a gift truly worth giving.

Don't Be Afraid to Try New Things

ROSE: When you're about to throw up from the stench, that's when they're done. Who wants some?

DOROTHY: Rose, if these had been offered to the Donner party, they still would have eaten each other.

It's easier to get into a rut than it is to get an MC for the Ladies Auxiliary Variety Show. Especially if you're not related to Bob Hope.

Rose is always happy to introduce her friends to a rich and often fish-based array of Scandinavia's oldest and most traditional appetizers, entrées, and treats. Though her dishes are not always to her roommates' liking, they've at least tried them, usually. Most often there are lots of leftovers on the serving trays, though some items, like her Sperhuven Krispies, have turned out to be surprisingly tasty. Similarly, when Rose's relationship with Miles becomes as boring as a tour of the Thimble Museum, they spice up their relationship and try skydiving. Likewise, after some hesitation, Dorothy manages to get out of her own same-old-same-old in the house and go perform at the Rusty Anchor. Blanche is always on the lookout for new positions, and Sophia looks for diversion in bowling, playing cards, and running races.

It's important, especially when you get older, to do what you can to keep yourself from getting stuck in a monotonous routine. Shaking up your days and nights (especially if you have some whipped cream) keeps things interesting, your mind active, and your body limber.

You're Never Too Old

SOPHIA: This is the kind of mistake you're supposed to make when you're nineteen. It gives me hope to think you can be just as dopey at eighty-two.

You're never too old to start something new.

Sophia's estranged best friend, Esther Weinstock, passes away and Sophia is reluctant to go to the funeral because she blames Esther's husband, Max, for gambling away his and Sal's business decades ago. At Esther's funeral, Max finally reveals the truth. . . . Sal gambled away the money and Max took the blame to keep Sal and Sophia together. Max's secret act of kindness touches Sophia, and they reconcile. Days after the funeral, Dorothy makes a shocking discovery when she goes to Sophia's room. Their years-long hostility on the streets of Brooklyn has turned into passion between the sheets in Miami—and talk of opening a pizza/knish stand on the boardwalk.

There's no age limit on love, friendship, and business—so go for it all!

Chosen Families Are Just as Valid as Families of Origin

NURSE: I said family only.

DOROTHY: You've never met this woman's family. They live in a place called St. Olaf. They fight over whether it's "macaroni and cheese" or "cheese and macaroni."

F amilies aren't always made from blood relations.

Sometimes, because of tragedy or circumstance, a person's biological family isn't available or able to provide them what they need. In those instances, family relationships must be found elsewhere: in a friend group, a mentor, or a community. In fact, because of any number of factors, some chosen families can be even stronger and more affirming than traditional family units.

Because hospitals only allow families in to see patients, Dorothy, Blanche, and Sophia are kept from seeing Rose as she's prepared for triple-bypass surgery. They're terrified, not only because Rose is sick, but because the medical staff won't provide them with any information. Rose's daughter Kirsten arrives and, after insisting that the Girls are no more than her mother's roommates, panics about how she's going to handle all the bills and therapies involved in Rose's recovery. When the Girls insist on helping to take care of Rose during her recovery, including mortgaging the house to pay for her care, Kirsten finally understands that their bond transcends being merely roommates or even friends.

Chosen families ground and comfort people living far from their biological or traditional families and can serve as a safe haven for those estranged or otherwise separated from their relatives. Even though they may be filled with nitwits (Scandinavian or otherwise), they're *your* nitwits and need to be celebrated and treasured for the security, love, and support they provide.

Friendship Is Forever

ROSE: I mean, what can you say about seven years of fights and laughter. Secrets. Cheesecake.

DOROTHY: Just that it's been very . . . Well, it's been an experience that I'll always keep very close to my heart. And that these are memories that I'll wrap myself in when the world gets cold and I forget that there are people who are warm and loving and . . .
I love you. Always.

No matter how you prepare for them, endings can be harder than a candy found at the bottom of a wicker purse.

Nobody would have ever thought Dorothy would be the first Golden Girl to remarry. And they'd be right. Though Sophia was *actually* the first, Dorothy's remarriage may certainly be the most memorable, not only because her marriage to Blanche's uncle Lucas ended the seven-year relationship of the four characters but also because it served as the ending of the series. Even though we all rooted for Dorothy to get her happy ending, the closing moments of the show were filled with as many tears as laughs. Along with Dorothy, Blanche, Rose, and Sophia, we were consoled by the fact that though the experience—or any experience—may be fleeting and final, true friendship endures.

Everything must, eventually, come to an end. But thanks to your memories (not to mention syndicated reruns and streaming services), you can revisit and enjoy your friends whenever you'd like.

More from the lanai